Joseph's Dreams

Storyline **Susan J. Davis**
Illustrations **Steven Butler**

Joseph lived with his father and brothers.
They lived in tents in the land of Canaan.

Joseph's mother had died but Joseph's
father, Jacob, loved him very much.

Joseph loved his family. He loved
his father and his brothers.

Jacob taught Joseph to love and worship the God of heaven.

When Joseph was a young man, Jacob gave him a beautiful coat of many colors.

Joseph loved his coat, but his brothers hated it.
"Father loves Joseph more than us!" they said.

One night, Joseph had a dream. He and his brothers were tying wheat into sheaves.

Joseph's sheaf stood up straight, and his brothers' sheaves bowed down before it.

Then Joseph had another dream. This time the sun, moon, and stars bowed down before him.

What did these dreams mean? Joseph was
sure that his dreams meant something.

Joseph told his brothers about the dreams. His brothers were angry. "Must we bow down to you?" they asked.

Joseph told his father about the dreams. "Must your brothers and I bow down to you?" asked Jacob.

Soon the grass was gone, so Joseph's brothers
took the sheep to find more grass.

They were gone so long that Jacob worried.
"Go find them," Jacob told Joseph.

Wearing his coat of many colors, Joseph
set out to find his brothers and the sheep.

Joseph looked and looked. Finally, a man told Joseph they had gone farther north.

Joseph's brothers saw him coming from far away.
They saw the coat of many colors.

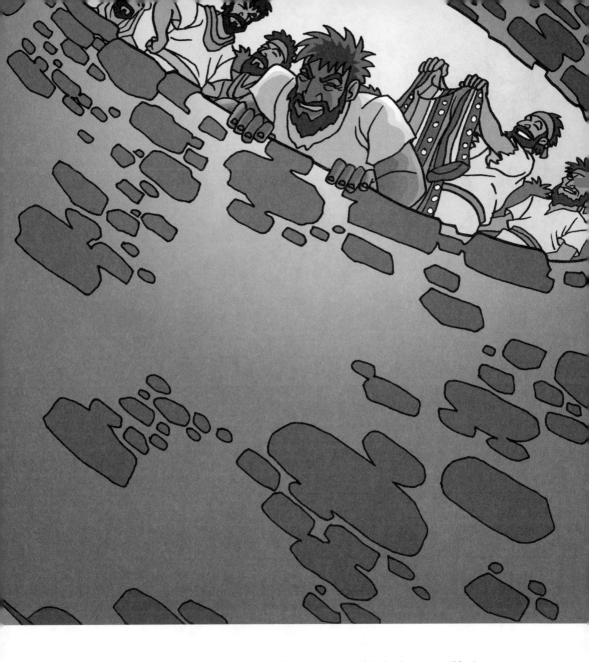

They grabbed Joseph, tore off his beautiful
coat, and threw him into a deep pit.

Some traders rode by on their way to Egypt.
The brothers sold Joseph to the traders.

Then they dipped Joseph's coat in blood. They told Jacob that an animal had killed Joseph.

On the way to Egypt, Joseph remembered
what his father had taught him.

Joseph vowed to worship the God of heaven, no matter what happened.

Joseph didn't know it yet, but God
had a plan for him in Egypt.